AQUATIC ANIMALS
IN THE WILD AND IN CAPTIVITY

Patricia Curtis

LODESTAR BOOKS

Dutton • New York

to Sasha and Louis Weiss

Library of Congress Cataloging-in-Publication Data

Curtis, Patricia, 1923–
 Aquatic animals: in the wild and in capivity / Patricia Curtis.—1st ed.
  p. cm.
 Includes index.
 Summary: Describes six representative aquatic habitats and the
animals that live in them, and discusses how modern aquariums recreate
those environments.
 ISBN 0-525-67384-9
 1. Aquariums, Public—Juvenile literature. 2. Aquatic animals—Juvenile
literature. 3. Aquariums, Public—United States—Juvenile literature.
[1. Aquatic animals. 2. Aquariums, Public.]
 I. Title.
 QL78.C87 1992
 590'.74'4—dc20   91-17010
                                                        CIP
                                                        AC

Published in the United States by Lodestar Books, an affiliate of
Dutton Children's Books, a division of Penguin Books USA Inc.,
375 Hudson Street, New York, New York 10014

Editor: Virginia Buckley

Designer: Keithley and Associates

Printed in Hong Kong   First Edition   10 9 8 7 6 5 4 3 2 1

Contents

Acknowledgments

My most heartfelt gratitude goes to Paul Loiselle, curator of freshwater fishes at the New York Aquarium. Throughout the preparation of this book, Dr. Loiselle made himself available to me with information and suggestions, and I was fortunate indeed to have his attention, encouragement, and expertise.

My warm thanks also to Karen Asis, of the American Association of Zoological Parks and Aquariums, for much help and valuable material.

To several good friends, my deep appreciation: Vicki Dennison for research; David Cupp and Jane Sapinsky for photographs; Helene Tetrault for her knowledge of birds; Ronnie Lutkins for untiring interest and companionship on research expeditions; and the Humane Society of the United States for photographs and information.

And for information or photos, many thanks to aquarists and other staff members at the following institutions: Dallas Aquarium; Memphis Zoo and Aquarium; Monterey Bay Aquarium; National Aquarium in Baltimore; Marine Mammal Commission, Washington, D.C.; Point Defiance Zoo & Aquarium, Tacoma; Scripps Aquarium-Museum, La Jolla; Vancouver Aquarium; Audubon Zoo, New Orleans; Brookfield Zoo, near Chicago; Cincinnati Zoo; Los Angeles Zoo; Minnesota Zoo, Apple Valley; National Zoo, Smithsonian Institution, Washington, D.C.; Pittsburgh Aviary; Saint Louis Zoo; Toledo Zoo; and Woodland Park Zoo, Seattle.

Animals and the New Aquariums

Our earth is called the water planet. Most of it is covered with water, which is the habitat of nearly all living things. Because we humans are land creatures, and the animals we know best also live on land, we don't realize that humans are members of a very small minority on earth.

We also tend to use the word "animal" only when we refer to mammals, but actually, all beings that move voluntarily, acquire and digest food, and have nervous systems that respond when stimulated are animals. The animal kingdom includes mammals, fish, birds, reptiles, and invertebrates (animals without backbones, such as insects, worms, oysters, and the like). Not only do most animals live in water, but over 90 percent of our fellow earth dwellers are invertebrates!

Aqua is the Latin word for water, and many of the terms we use in referring to water are derived from it—for example, the noun aquarium and the adjective aquatic. A curator, other scientist, or keeper at an aquarium is an aquarist. Another word you will hear in reference to animals of the water is marine, which means "of the sea."

Aquatic ecosystems may be fresh water, salt water, or a combination of both, called brackish. All three support animal life. Fish and a huge variety

Sea urchins, found along the bottom of all seas, are not plants but invertebrate animals about the size of oranges. Here, red and purple sea urchins share an aquarium exhibit with anemones.

of invertebrates get their life-sustaining oxygen in the fresh or salt waters of their habitats. Some mammals, such as whales and dolphins, also live in water. Unlike fish, they must come to the surface to breathe air, but they cannot live out of water.

In addition to the animals that live *in* water, there are those that make their homes along the coasts and shores and in swamps and wetlands. These mammals, birds, and reptiles breathe air and spend their time both in water and on land. But they must be near water to nest, breed, or feed themselves. And even land animals, including ourselves, must have water in order to live.

Like zoos, the first public aquariums existed solely as places of recreation, where people could go just to gawk at the odd life-forms that live in water. But in modern aquariums, including those that are part of zoos, you not only meet wonderful and strange aquatic animals but also learn about their behavior, characteristics, and natural habitats.

The tundra swan, also called the whistling swan, is over four feet long and has a powerful voice. It summers in the arctic regions of North America but winters on our lakes and sounds.

At aquariums today, scientists study the creatures of our water world. Researchers know that fish have brains, and that they can learn, remember, taste, and smell; they can "hear" by feeling waves and vibrations in the water. While fish don't have voices, they can make noise with their bodies. Though all fish get dissolved oxygen from the water through their gills, a few species can also breathe air. Fish sleep, not with their eyes shut but in a quiet state. Some are carnivores (meat eaters); others browse on vegetation.

Besides fish, aquariums exhibit mammals, birds, reptiles, amphibians, and those invertebrates that are dependent on water. The new aquariums are living museums. They give us a glimpse of what our true earth and its inhabitants are like.

Many aquariums and good-sized zoos have exhibits of entire watery ecosystems, such as rain forests, polar shores, swamps, or marshes, and display together those creatures that live in them. These exhibits have names such as Amazon Gallery, Louisiana Swamp, Gulf of Mexico, Discov-

The capybara, a native of the riverbanks of Central and South America, is the world's largest rodent and can weigh over 200 pounds. A gentle vegetarian, it squeaks and whistles like a guinea pig.

ery Cove, The Estuaries, or Rocky Shores. Detailed signs explain them to us. And equally important, these exhibits often alert us to the present sorry state of much of our earth's waters. The New England Aquarium, for example, has an exhibit devoted to Boston Harbor, showing the public what it means when a major harbor is ruined by sewage and garbage.

In the past, we humans didn't think much about what we did to the seas, lakes, and rivers. We took it for granted that water was plentiful, so we didn't worry about wasting it. We assumed that aquatic plant and animal life would always be there.

Now we are beginning to realize that, in many places, this precious commodity, water, is disappearing or is becoming so polluted it cannot support life. The animals and plants of some water ecosystems have already either died off or contain such high levels of toxin in their bodies that the creatures who eat them become poisoned.

Since modern times, nearly all the land areas of the earth have belonged to someone—either a government, a group of persons, or an individual. This is not true of the seas. Nations do claim the water bordering their coasts, but the open seas, the so-called international waters, are regarded as belonging to nobody. Therefore, nations for the most part have felt free to pollute them and to kill whatever lives in them. But now we know that whatever goes into the water miles out to sea eventually washes up on someone's shores. Depleting the seas of fish or other animals, or dumping millions of tons of waste into the sea, affects the land and humans as well. The condition of the seas is an international concern.

The animals that depend on certain bodies of water give accurate signals about the health of those waters. When a river is polluted, when a pond or marsh dries up, its animals begin to die or, if they can, go elsewhere to seek purer water. Human beings would do well to pay attention. One of the most important things a good aquarium teaches us is what we can do to protect and conserve the planet's waters everywhere.

Today, as people become increasingly interested in aquatic animals, new aquariums are being built. Older aquariums are being expanded or improved. Many zoos are enlarging their aquariums, or adding exhibits of aquatic ecosystems. An organization that has influenced the upgrading of both zoos and aquariums is the American Association of Zoological Parks and Aquariums (AAZPA), founded by zoo and aquarium professionals in 1972. This organization sets standards and guidelines for the display of captive wildlife. In order to be a member of the AAZPA and become accredited, a zoo or aquarium has to meet those standards.

AAZPA members also hold meetings, share information, and coordinate efforts to save endangered species. The better zoos and aquariums have begun to do important work toward saving many endangered wild creatures of both land and sea from extinction.

One program sponsored by the AAZPA is the Species Survival Plan (SSP). Certain species (fifty-six at present) of mammals, birds, reptiles, and fish that are in the greatest danger of becoming extinct have been selected.

A colorful reef fish, the Australian orangetail damsel, three to four inches long, is a loner and doesn't school like some other fish. Males, however, are aggressively territorial and will vigorously protect eggs in their nests.

Many zoos and aquariums are cooperating in breeding these species to assure that they don't vanish forever from the earth. One goal of the SSP is to breed enough healthy members of a species so that some can be released, where possible, back into the wild.

The better aquariums today are concentrating on building entire naturalistic ecosystems. A popular exhibit at most good aquariums is the coral reef, which shows off the beauty of the fish and other creatures of this complex ecosystem. When a few bright-colored reef fish circle endlessly in a plain tank, you learn little about their natural lives or their true habitat. But in a good exhibit, you see the fish, and many creatures and plants they coexist with, behaving normally in a true coral reef setting. Water temperature, sea salt, light, oxygen, and even wave motion imitate the real thing. Signs tell you about the animals and why it is important to protect the earth's natural reefs everywhere.

Advanced engineering technology, creative design, and greater knowledge of aquatic life have made it possible to build truly realistic exhibits in which animals can live comfortably. An aquarium must be designed to include machinery for continual cleaning and filtering of water, yet there must be no noise or vibration of the pumps because that would disturb the animals. Waves and water currents must be created mechanically. Water and air temperatures must be controlled and constantly monitored to be sure they are right for the different animals. Rocks and plants, real or man-made, must be positioned for the comfort of the animals as well as for the realism of the exhibit. One zoo that has an exhibit of tiny rain forest frogs even plays tape recordings of thunderstorms from time to time to make the frogs feel at home.

One amphibian of the disappearing rain forests of Madagascar is called a tomato frog, and it's easy to see why.

Light must be arranged to resemble what the animals are used to, yet allow visitors to see them. Because some aquatic animals live in the wild at depths where there is little light, their tanks in an aquarium cannot be brightly lighted. Instead, the galleries themselves are dimly lighted, making the exhibits easier to see. Some aquariums provide raised seating so visitors can sit and enjoy the constantly moving drama within an exhibit.

For its huge variety of animals, an aquarium must supply a wide range of highly nutritious food: crickets, flies, fish, meat, shellfish, squid, krill (tiny shrimplike creatures), vegetables, and worms. Some animals are very particular and will eat only live prey; some won't eat fish if it has been frozen. The carnivores need a certain amount of vegetable matter as well as meat. Many aquariums grow much of the food their animals eat (fruit flies, for instance). A lot of people are kept very busy supplying the food for animals as varied as tadpoles and sharks, ducks and otters, turtles and sea lions.

Many valuable animals in an aquarium are difficult to care for. Aquarists must know how to keep them healthy. There are only a few veterinarians who specialize in marine mammals; there are no veterinarians for fish. If a fish at an aquarium appears ill, a fish pathologist may be called. That's a scientist who studies diseases of fish. A fish is difficult to treat. It can be given medicine by injection, or immersed in medicated baths, but that's about all that can be done.

Some aquariums have divers who swim in the tanks and feed the fish, clean the exhibits, and talk to visitors through underwater microphones. Others have microphones arranged so visitors can hear the sounds made by the animals, even the fish. Some keepers form familiar, affectionate relationships with the animals in their care, almost like those that some zookeepers enjoy with land animals.

This book is divided into six representative aquatic habitats, and animals who live together in each one are described together. You'll read about them as you might see them at a modern aquarium or at a good aquatic exhibit in a zoo. By learning something about how these animals live in their natural habitats, you'll have more pleasure when seeing them in naturalistic exhibits.

Animals of the Freshwater Lakes and Wetlands

ost of us in North America live not very far from a body of fresh water—a lake or at least a pond. If it is healthy, its waters and shores are teeming with life.

Lakes are fed by rivers, streams, or underground springs and may be deep; if they are very wide, they usually have waves. Ponds are shallow by comparison and tend to have a uniform water temperature—the same in the middle as at the shore, and more or less the same at every depth. Ponds are usually fed by rainfall or by water that runs off the surrounding land. Depending on climate, lakes and ponds may freeze solid in winter or dry up in periods of drought.

Freshwater wetlands—swamps, marshes, and bogs—have shallow water and wet, spongy soil, with grasses, rushes, and cattails growing in them. Wetlands extend around the edges of larger bodies of water and are good water storage areas. If a lake or river overflows, wetlands act as a basin, holding the water and preventing the flooding of nearby land. These vital ecosystems are home or nesting place to thousands of species of animals, and essential havens where migrating birds can stop to rest, feed, and drink.

Birds of the lakes and wetlands include the swimmers: ducks, swans, and geese, for example, and loons and grebes, who are great swimmers and divers but so thoroughly adapted to water that they can barely walk on land. Other wetland birds are the long-legged waders, such as herons, ibises, and spoonbills.

———

Spoonbills are nearly three feet tall and named for the shape of their bill. When feeding, a spoonbill stands in shallow water and sweeps its head from side to side underwater, scooping up insects and other creatures. To feed its young, a parent opens its bill and lets the chick thrust its own spoon-shaped bill deep within to get partially digested food.

Various species of spoonbills live in mostly warm climates near water throughout the world, but the showy roseate spoonbill is found only in North and South America. These birds were hunted almost to extinction for their feathers and plumes, used as trimmings and decorations. Today, loss of habitat, particularly the mangrove swamps, makes the roseate spoonbill's future in the wild uncertain.

Both aquariums and zoos are likely to have pond or swamp exhibits, or special aquatic bird displays. If an exhibit is thickly wooded, you may have to peek between the branches and shrubs to see the birds. Look near the water. Wading birds spend a lot of time standing still on their long legs, preening their feathers.

Many lake and wetland ecosystems and the wildlife that depend on them are in danger today. As cities have grown up in the dry areas of our country, water to supply them has been diverted from the streams that have fed natural lakes for millions of years. This lowers the water level of the lakes, reduces the amount of water available to wildlife, and changes the chemical composition of the water. In some places wildlife that formerly lived in or around such lakes has disappeared.

Lake habitats are upset by shore development, for when people build houses near the nesting places of water birds, the birds have no place to nest, or their nests are destroyed.

Wetlands are lost when farmers convert them into cropland. In recent years, our government has been urging farmers not to do this, often buying their wetland acres in order to preserve them. Many farmers object, and this complicated issue is hotly debated.

One threat to freshwater ecosystems today is acid rain. When poisonous exhausts from automobiles, factories, and power plants go into the air, they are absorbed by clouds and return to earth in rainfall. Acid rain falling on a lake, pond, stream, or wetland makes the water toxic and can either kill

Audubon Zoo

A roseate spoonbill chick seeks supper from its parent's open bill.

the creatures that live in the water or cause such high levels of poison in their bodies that animals who eat them die. In other words, the toxins in acid rain go right up the food chain.

For years, conservationists have been urging our government to make industrial plants stop putting poisonous gases into the air and to limit the concentrations of toxins in automobile exhausts, but so far, little has been done to stop the creation of acid rain.

———

Fish of any given lake, isolated by the land around their habitat, are often unique. Fish in lakes west of the Rocky Mountains, for example, are different from similar species in lakes in the eastern United States.

One large family of freshwater fish found in many parts of the world is the cichlids. In Lake Victoria, in east Africa, a group called Haplochromis (hap-lo-kro-mis) has evolved since the lake was formed about 250,000 years ago. These beautiful cichlids are different in looks and behavior from any others on earth.

Around forty years ago, some misguided authorities introduced another kind of fish, the Nile perch, into the lake to "improve" the fishing. The Nile perch is a large carnivore; haplochromine cichlids are small, three to five inches long, and eat both small aquatic animals and vegetation. In a short time, the perch ate virtually all the haplochromines. The entire ecosystem of the lake was upset by the introduction of that foreign fish. Many haplochromine cichlids are now extinct in Lake Victoria, but about a dozen species are being bred by aquariums in a cooperative program.

The females of all haplochromine species are mouth brooders, which refers to their way of caring for their eggs. After a male has selected a breeding place and been joined by a female, the female lays her eggs. She immediately takes the eggs into her mouth. They are fertilized by the male, and then the female swims away, keeping the eggs in her mouth, safe from predators. In the wild, a brooding female will seek out a quiet beach where she can hide and avoid predators. In an aquarium, she is usually removed to a tank by herself, for her comfort and safety.

The little blue and gold Lake Victoria haplochromine cichlid hasn't been seen in the wild since the large Nile perch was introduced into its habitat.

In three weeks, the eggs—usually numbering fifty or so—hatch, and the female releases the fry (baby fish) from her mouth. For perhaps a week after that, she stays near them, and if they are threatened or scared, she lets them back in her mouth. Since she doesn't eat during the time she carries the eggs in her mouth, aquarists usually keep the female in isolation for a week or so afterward while she regains her strength.

The male is a fierce fighter. Two warring males ram each other mouth to mouth, grasp each other's lips, and engage in a tug-of-war that may tear away parts of their lips. Finally one gives up and swims away, indicating by his behavior and a change in color that he is submissive, which may be the signal that stops the victor from killing him.

In an aquarium, haplochromine cichlids need lots of room; rockwork caves to hide in; and vegetation, algae (very simple aquatic organisms), and insects to eat. You can see species of this and other Lake Victoria fish in freshwater exhibits in the many aquariums participating in the plan to save them.

One animal, the North American beaver, not only lives in our freshwater lakes and ponds but often changes them to suit itself. Most important, this animal creates much-needed wetlands.

Beavers are large rodents, three to four feet long and usually weighing about forty-five pounds. Their diet is mainly bark, twigs, and branches, especially of willow and poplar trees. They have sharp, very strong teeth in both their upper and lower jaws, which they use to shave a tree trunk or branch. In just a few minutes, a beaver can fell a tree with a trunk that's five inches in diameter.

Being a mammal, a beaver of course breathes air, but it can stay underwater for long periods, sometimes as long as fifteen minutes. When it dives, it automatically closes its ears and nose, and a transparent membrane moves over its eyes to keep out the water. Its hind feet are webbed, and it has a large, flat tail used as a rudder when swimming and as a prop when squatting on its haunches to chew the bark of a tree. The tail also serves as a warning device. When disturbed, a beaver loudly smacks the water with its tail, causing all beavers within hearing distance immediately to dive into the water and disappear.

Beavers stay with one mate for life, and in spring produce a litter of three or four babies, which are called kits. A beaver family builds its dome-shaped lodge of branches, twigs, grasses, and mud, roughly thirteen feet in diameter and two or three feet tall, with a dry sleeping platform inside. The lodge is entered from underwater. During the summer the animals build a raft of branches under the lodge; these serve as their winter food supply. Beavers keep their home in good repair and use it for years. Anyone who has seen a strong, well-constructed beaver lodge has to admit that this animal is an expert engineer.

While early Native Americans hunted beavers for food and especially for their beautiful thick, soft fur, those people did not threaten the animals' survival as a species. But when white trappers of the nineteenth century pushed into the wilderness to harvest beaver pelts for the fashion trade, and

Minnesota Zoo

The beaver is the world's second largest rodent. Here, a beaver apparently considers the bark of a birch log very tasty.

encouraged the Indians to do the same, so many millions of beavers were killed that the species almost disappeared. It was saved only when the fashion for beaver hats declined.

A beaver lodge in a lake, pond, or stream acts as a dam, diverting water and creating wetlands. In many places, these dams cause water to be stored instead of flooding the surrounding land. Also, when beavers run out of food around one place, they move on and set up housekeeping in another area. Their abandoned lodges eventually sink and provide rich bottomland that over time becomes meadows.

However, sometimes a beaver dam causes water to flood a road or railroad track, or interferes with human activity in some way. Then the game wardens shoot the beavers. Also, they are designated a game species in most states, so people can trap them for profit. State wildlife agencies get income from selling hunting and trapping licenses.

Though beavers are aquatic animals, you'll most often find them in zoos rather than in aquariums, but they are always provided with a pool. A number of zoos have underwater windows so you can watch the animals busily carrying on their activities. Some zoos, such as the Minnesota, give their beavers fresh poplar branches every day to use in building their own lodge and keeping it in repair. Underwater television cameras in their lodge let you see the animals at home. The beavers also use the branches to build their own storage place for food. They are fed rodent chow supplemented with raw vegetables and apples, as well as poplar branches.

Most zoos that exhibit beavers keep at least a pair, male and female, who sometimes produce kits.

The word amphibian refers to the class of animals that breathe air, live both on land and in water, and lay their eggs in water. The eggs hatch tadpoles who must live in water and breathe through gills, as fish do, until they develop lungs and turn into air-breathers. Frogs, toads, and salamanders are amphibians.

These animals are vertebrates, but cold-blooded, which means their body temperature is the same as that of their environment. (The body temperature of warm-blooded animals like ourselves is more or less constant, independent of the environment.)

The skin of amphibians is water-permeable, capable of being penetrated by water. This makes them highly sensitive to their environment. Scientists consider them particularly good barometers of the condition of the environment. Today, many of the world's populations of amphibians are dying off, another warning that we humans should stop polluting.

Toads and frogs look a lot alike, but toads can only hop, while frogs can leap. Toads have dry, bumpy skin. Frogs have moist, smooth skin, which must be kept wet or damp.

One group of tiny, bright-colored frogs carries its defense system in its skin. Called poison arrow frogs, or poison dart frogs, they produce a mucus in their skin that painfully burns the mouth of any creature that bites them. A few kinds of poison arrow frogs produce a mucus that is highly toxic, and the native people of Central and South America, where these frogs live, used to dip the tips of their arrows in it. Depending on the kind of frog, the toxin could kill a bird, monkey, or even a larger animal. Today, medical researchers are studying the toxin for possible medicinal uses for humans.

For reasons that are not yet known, blue poison arrow frogs born in captivity don't produce toxin in their skin. Scientists studying them wonder if there is something in the animals' wild environment or diet that stimulates them to produce the toxin.

Saint Louis Zoo

The tiny blue poison arrow frog is from the rain forests of Suriname, a country on the northeast coast of South America.

The National Aquarium in Baltimore is a leader in the breeding of blue poison arrow frogs. Researchers weren't having much luck getting them to breed until they found something the frogs liked to lay their eggs in. The aquarists snapped the bottoms off two-liter soda bottles, cut a little door in the side, and made little huts. The tiny frogs have been laying eggs in them ever since.

The strawberry poison arrow frog, one of the prettiest, lives in the rain forests of Central America. The female has an unusual parenting behavior. She lays her eggs on the ground, and as soon as the tadpoles are hatched, she takes each one on her back (nobody knows how the little tadpole is able to stick to her back) and carries it to a bromeliad, a tropical plant with showy flowers. She puts the tadpole into the water-filled cup of a bromeliad flower. Then she returns every few days, and when the tadpole wiggles its tail to show that it's still alive, she backs into the water and lays a few nonfertile eggs for it to eat.

Aquariums and zoos that have rain forest exhibits are likely to have at least one species of poison arrow frogs.

In nature, bright color means one of two things: Come closer or stay away. Flowers use their color to attract birds and bees to pollinate them. The males of some bird species have bright feathers to attract females. But in some other animals, bright color means "Touch me and die!" Certain snakes and lizards, for example, as well as poison arrow frogs, are good examples. Their beautiful color seems to say to predators "If you eat me, we're both dead," and most predators take the hint.

Lakes and wetlands are the home of many kinds of turtles, the most primitive of modern-day reptiles. Today's turtles haven't changed much from those that lived 200 million years ago. There are some 250 species of freshwater and sea turtles. They range in size from the little ones you might keep as pets in a terrarium to the giant sea turtles that weigh 800 to 900 pounds.

Sea turtles are endangered, which means there are so few of them in the wild that they are in danger of becoming extinct. One reason for their decline is the method of netting that shrimp fishermen use. Sea turtles get caught in the nets along with the shrimp, and they drown. But the main reason is human habitation along beaches where the females lay their eggs. Normally, when the hatchlings emerge from the eggs, they head right for the sea, guided by the sky light reflected on the water. But where lighted houses or highways border the beaches, the newly hatched sea turtles become confused and waddle in the wrong direction to their death.

Some states such as Florida and Texas do not allow development of beaches where sea turtles lay their eggs. Sometimes people come to the beach when the eggs are hatching and carry the babies to the sea. And in some places there are Head Start programs in which the turtle eggs are gathered and kept for hatching in captivity. After a year, when the turtles are safely grown, they are released.

One sea turtle, the hawksbill, is killed for its beautiful shell, called tortoise shell, which is made into jewelry, combs, and ornamental objects. Environmental organizations such as Greenpeace and the World Wildlife

Fund are working to save sea turtles, and a few aquariums are breeding them.

Most aquariums and zoos have turtle exhibits. You might also find turtles in reptile displays, or in swamp exhibits.

The alligator snapping turtle is a resident of our American southern freshwater swamps. Its name comes from a mistaken notion held by the early settlers in America. The settlers were familiar with the common snapping turtle that weighs between 50 and 100 pounds, but they were puzzled by the fearsome-looking snapper that can weigh as much as 200. The settlers decided the big one must be a cross between a snapping turtle and an alligator.

David Schleser/Dallas Aquarium

An alligator snapping turtle, like all turtles, has no teeth, but its sharp bony jaws do very well in seizing and eating its prey.

Eventually people learned that turtles don't mate with alligators, and vice versa, but the name alligator snapping turtle stuck.

The common snapping turtle captures its food—fish, shellfish, frogs—with a fast strike of its powerful jaws. The alligator snapping turtle is less aggressive but catches prey by deception. This animal stays very still in the water, opens its mouth, and wiggles its tongue like a pink worm. When a fish or frog swims up close to investigate the "worm," that's when the turtle quickly snaps its mouth shut. Even in captivity, this turtle may display its tongue. One 140-pound alligator snapping turtle at the Memphis Zoo aquarium, living in a tank by himself and fed plenty of thawed frozen fish, sometimes sits wiggling his tongue, apparently hunting by instinct.

Animals of the Rivers

Rivers thread their way across all the continents of the world. Look at a map, and you'll see that, except in the deserts, rivers wide and narrow flow for many miles to reach the seas. They often move swiftly through deep canyons, or sometimes meander slowly across plains. Rivers support a variety of animal life, both in their waters and on their banks. Except where they reach the seas and mix with tidal flows of salt water, rivers are freshwater systems.

Many rivers are in trouble today, polluted by sewage, industrial waste, and acid rain. When trees are removed by logging, the bare earth washes into rivers, filling them with soil. Mining near rivers clogs the water with soil. Every dam, factory, recreation area, or house along a river affects the quality of the water and of course its wildlife. But in some places today, environmental protection agencies and private organizations of concerned people work to defend rivers against activities that will damage them.

————

The hippopotamus, which you'll see in zoos rather than in aquariums, is a river dweller. An ancient Greek historian gave this animal its name, which means "river horse." However, it is not related to the horse—it belongs to the large family of even-toed animals such as camels, giraffes,

A female hippopotamus gives birth underwater, usually to a single baby, which weighs about forty pounds. The baby can swim before it walks, and climbs onto its mother's back for sunbathing.

pigs, and deer. A strict vegetarian, the hippo eats grasses and other vegetation growing in the river or along its banks.

In their natural African habitat, hippos spend most of their time loafing in shallow rivers or wallowing in the mud on the banks. Their skin is very sensitive and must be kept moist; it cracks if it gets too dry. Their eyes, ears, and nostrils are on the top of their head, and often that's all you see of them when they're in the water. A good zoo provides them with a pool deep enough to completely submerge in, and a sand bank with plenty of mud. At the Woodland Park Zoo, the hippos' stable is even equipped with overhead sprinklers to keep the animals' skin moist overnight.

Despite their enormous bulk (some weigh over two tons—that's more than 4000 pounds), hippos can gallop on land when they have to, and they are rather graceful in water, paddling along or tiptoeing on the river bottom. Hippos can hold their breath underwater for up to ten minutes. At the Toledo Zoo you can watch them underwater through glass windows.

Hippos are normally calm but unpredictable. Most people avoid them in the wild, and zookeepers treat them with respect. When frightened or angry, a hippo usually tries intimidation first, by opening its mouth wide to display its impressive teeth and long tusks. Young hippos play-fight, but adult males fight seriously over females.

Many zoos have hippos, usually a male and one or two females. Babies are born occasionally. Some years ago, a young hippo named Kubwasana, who had been hand-raised because his mother neglected him, arrived at the Woodland Park Zoo, in Seattle. Kubwasana immediately adopted his keeper as his mother and followed him around like a dog. Whenever the keeper sat down in Kubwasana's pen, the hippo put his head in the man's lap. When he grew up, however, Kubwasana transferred his affections to a female hippopotamus, and today, some years later, he shares a habitat at the zoo with two females, Gertrude and Water Lily.

———————

In the slow-moving rivers and streams of the southern United States and northern Mexico lives a huge fish that so resembles an alligator that it's called the alligator gar. Its body resembles a cigar and is covered with hard, diamond-shaped scales. It looks as if it has been left over from prehistoric times, and indeed it has existed almost unchanged for more than 100 million years. Considering that we human beings have been around for only a few million years, that's old!

An alligator gar takes in oxygen through gills, as nearly all other fish do, but it also has an air bladder that enables it to breathe air at the water's surface. It can live in shallow, murky waters where other fish might die from lack of oxygen.

An aggressive predator, it will lurk quietly just under the surface like its reptile namesake, then dash suddenly to capture other fish, birds, reptiles, worms, mollusks, and shellfish in its sharp, pointed teeth. In an aquarium,

The alligator gar, six to ten feet long, is such an ancient species that it is considered a living fossil.

an alligator gar is exhibited only with other very large fish, for obvious reasons! It is fed mostly thawed frozen small fish called smelts.

Though there are scary stories about the fierce alligator gar, there aren't any proven accounts of a person being attacked by one in the water. However, a fisherman who lands one of them has to be careful not to get bitten. If you see one of these big fish in an aquarium, you're not likely to forget it.

The piranha, another predatory river fish, has an even worse reputation. It has very strong jaws and sharp little teeth. It lives in the shallow basins, streams, and canals of the Orinoco and Amazon rivers, in South America. It is a relatively small fish, ranging in size from ten to fourteen inches, but according to folklore, schools of piranhas can reduce humans and other animals to skeletons in a few minutes.

In truth, people living along these rivers bathe in the waters all the time, because piranhas won't attack unless they are starving or harassed.

The aggressive red-bellied piranha has a face like a bulldog's and a mouthful of sharp little teeth.

But if these fish find themselves trapped in a pool or pond where they can't get enough to eat, they will attack anything, including one another. In aquariums, they are fed pieces of fish, live minnows, chunks of shrimp, meat, and sometimes dead mice.

Aquariums and zoos with rain forest or Amazon exhibits often have a tank of piranhas. Many people have heard about these ferocious fish and enjoy seeing them (safely confined, of course, in a tank).

If you were asked to name the largest river-dwelling reptile, you'd think immediately of an alligator or crocodile. These animals belong to a group called crocodilians. Other crocodilians are the caimans of South America and the gavials, or gharials, of India and Pakistan.

Crocodilians in many parts of the world are threatened by a number of human activities, the main one being destruction of their habitats. Pollution of the water by insecticides and other industrial chemicals, disruption of nesting areas by back-up from dams, destruction of forests, which causes soil to erode—all these take a toll. In addition, many crocodilians are killed for their skins, which are used to make fancy leather goods. In some places people eat their eggs. Gavials in particular are rare and endangered in their natural habitat.

You can see alligators, crocodiles, and caimans of various kinds in many zoos and aquariums, but only a very few have gavials. In Jungle World, the Bronx Zoo's rain forest, the gharials, as they are called there, paddle in the man-made river and lounge on the bank. You can sit in front of a glass window and watch them swimming underwater.

If they have to defend themselves, gavials use their tails to knock down their enemy, and then they bite. But they are timid and retiring by nature, and if threatened, prefer to slither into the water to get away.

Like other crocodilians, gavials often stay submerged in water with only the tips of their noses exposed for air. On land, they are somewhat awkward, but when disturbed, they can raise their bodies on their stumpy legs and run fast for short distances.

At a roadside zoo in Florida, a crowd of alligators in a plain dirt pen can look forward to only a short life span.

When male gavials are eleven or twelve years old, they grow knobs on their long snouts. This one lives in a zoo's lush rain forest where he has sun and shade, a sandy beach, a pool to swim in, and females to keep him company.

When a female gavial wants to lay eggs, she digs a hole in the mud of the riverbank. She guards the nest while the eggs incubate, about eighty days. When the offspring in the shells are ready to hatch, they squeak as if calling to the mother. She responds by breaking the shells and carrying the babies in her mouth to the water. She then swims with the hatchlings for a while, until they are ready to be on their own.

Gavials play an important role in their wild ecosystem because they feed not only on fish but on carrion—the bodies of dead fish or other animals—thus helping clean up the rivers, streams, or lakes they live in.

Animals of the Estuaries and Salt Marshes

long the boundaries of continents and islands, where land and sea merge, or at the mouths of rivers, where fresh and salt water join, there are rich and important aquatic ecosystems. Many kinds of animals live in these relatively shallow waters or on the land at the edge of the water.

The mouths of rivers are called estuaries. Because the fresh water of the rivers and the salt water of the seas become mixed, estuaries are part fresh and part salt, or brackish. Many species are uniquely adapted to this kind of water.

When the flow of water from a river is slow, it deposits much sediment as it meets the sea. The incoming tides flood the land around the mouth of the river, forming marshes with grasses growing in the water. Certain species of fish, crabs, and shellfish—such as oysters and clams—live in these waters, attracting shore birds and migratory birds.

Many of the world's estuaries and salt marshes are being lost to agriculture, building, trash dumps, or recreational beaches. Also, these areas are increasingly affected by pollutants. When industrial wastes are emptied into rivers and reach the estuaries, they are continually recycled as the tides flow in and out. This repeated contamination of the waters by pollutants has extremely harmful effects on the animal and plant life.

Most aquariums have estuary, salt marsh, or tide pool exhibits, with detailed explanations of them. There is usually a touch pool where you can pick up some of the creatures. Many aquariums and zoos also exhibit birds of brackish water habitats.

Some birds of salt marsh habitats have long, narrow bills specially fashioned for prying shellfish out of their shells. One such bird is the avocet The European avocet is white, with distinct black markings. The American avocet, found in western North America, has a brick-red head, neck, and chest. Both species have unusual bills, which curve up instead of down.

An avocet feeds rather like a spoonbill, walking rapidly along in shallow water swinging its slightly open bill from side to side along the bottom, using it like a scoop. In the wild, it eats crustaceans, insects, worms, and other small marsh creatures. At an aquarium or zoo, avocets may feed this way in the water, or they may eat from a feeding tray. Some keepers put the birds' food in clam shells on the sand, which looks natural to birds and visitors alike. Avocets usually share an exhibit with other birds. They are given a mixture of chopped hard-boiled egg, chopped fish, meat, puppy chow, and other foods, and each species picks out whatever it likes best.

Avocets stand sixteen to eighteen inches tall and are strictly ground dwellers. Unlike the spoonbills and herons, they have webbed feet, like ducks, which would cause them a problem if they tried to perch in a tree. But when they wade into deep

Jane Sapinsky

The avocet has webbed feet that allow it to wade with ease on a muddy or sandy bottom or on soggy marshland.

water, they can swim. They can even upend themselves like ducks to get morsels of food from the bottom.

In the wild, avocets engage in a remarkable courtship display. As many as a dozen males and females do a sort of dance together, in intricate formations, often in a circle. Communicating with one another through head movements, they keep in perfect step and rhythm. After a while, by some secret signal, they stop and select individual mates.

Male and female build a nest together in low vegetation near water and take turns sitting on the eggs. Chicks hatch in a little over three weeks and are cared for by both parents until they are ready to be on their own.

Jane Sapinsky

If you see three birds but only four legs standing in the water in this zoo pond, that's because a flamingo sometimes rests on one leg with the other tucked up under its body.

The **flamingo**, nearly five feet tall with elegant pink plumage, is surely one of the superstars among aquatic birds at zoos and aquariums. On its long legs, it looks like a wading bird, but its true relatives are the swans and geese. In fact, when flamingo chicks hatch, they take to the water early and swim like goslings. The chicks don't even look much like their parents— they hatch white, turn gray, and stay gray for about a year before they become pink.

The flamingo has a unique feeding technique. It submerges its head and uses its tongue to pump water into its scoop-shaped bill, then filters the water like a sieve, leaving small insects, crustaceans, and vegetable matter in its bill.

Wild flamingos live in brackish habitats in South America, Europe, and Asia, in flocks of several hundred. They are such social birds that in captivity they won't breed unless they are kept in fairly good-sized flocks. Zoo Atlanta created a habitat for its flamingos just inside the entrance, so they are the first thing visitors see, and they make a spectacular display.

————

One salt marsh dweller, the hermit crab, protects itself from hungry predators by never leaving home. This little animal takes up residence in an abandoned shell, usually that of a snail or other mollusk, and carries it everywhere it goes. As the crab grows, its shell house becomes too small, so from time to time, it has to leave to find a bigger one. While house-hunting, it is of course vulnerable to many predators. It may fight other crabs for an empty shell, or even try to evict another hermit crab from its adopted shell.

Full-grown hermit crabs are about six inches long. They eat tiny sea creatures, both living and dead. Though some species can crawl about on land for short periods of time, they lay their eggs in the water, and the female carries the eggs under her abdomen until they hatch.

Jessie Cohen/National Zoo, Smithsonian Institution

This hermit crab has taken up residence in the shell of a whelk, a mollusk often found in shallow waters.

Hermit crabs live in all seas, not just in the shallow marshes but at all depths. At some zoos, you might find them in an invertebrate exhibit. At an aquarium, it's fun to watch them creeping along carrying their shell houses on the bottom of a tank, or in a salt marsh or tide pool exhibit.

In the animal kingdom, the role of the father varies greatly when it comes to parenting. In a few mammal species, such as humans, wolves, coyotes, wild dogs, and some monkeys, fathers are known to help raise their young. Most bird fathers, however, do an equal share in incubating eggs and feeding the chicks. But in many species of fish, the fathers do virtually *all* the parenting! They build the nest, guard the eggs, and take care of the fry.

One of these species is a tiny but spunky fish called the three-spined stickleback, named for the tiny spikes on its back. This two- to three-inch fish lives among the aquatic weeds of brackish marshes and tide pools throughout North America, Europe, and Asia. In an aquarium, you're likely to see sticklebacks in a tide pool or marsh exhibit.

Breeding is a complicated activity for a male stickleback. His belly turns bright red to attract females. He establishes a territory for himself,

John Brill

This male stickleback, only two inches long, would fiercely defend his nest against any creature that threatened it.

becoming aggressive toward other male sticklebacks who swim near, and gets busy building an elaborate nest. He makes a ball of plant material—leaves, twigs, and stems—cementing it together with a sticky substance from his own body. When he's satisfied with the ball, he anchors it by attaching it to underwater grasses. Then he tunnels into it, twirling around inside to pack the sides of the nest firmly.

When a female filled with eggs swims by, the male lures her by performing a sort of zigzag dance toward his nest. If she is ready to accept him and lay her eggs, she goes into the nest. Once she has laid her eggs, the female leaves, and that's it for parenthood as far as she is concerned. The rest is up to him. He may try to induce another female or two also to lay eggs in his nest.

Now the male stickleback fertilizes the eggs and proceeds to stand guard at the entrance to the nest. He doesn't sleep or even swim away to eat. With his fins he fans oxygen to the maturing eggs. He will attack fish much larger than himself if they threaten the eggs. After about a week, the eggs hatch, but the father keeps the fry in the nest to mature for another week. If one ventures out, he chases it, sucks it into his mouth, and blows it back into the nest. After another week, though, the young fish are old enough to leave, and the father can end his vigil. He may resume his regular life, or he may repair his nest and repeat the whole spawning process.

If an aquarium wants to breed sticklebacks, it provides nesting material and lets nature take its course.

Animals of the Coasts

 he waters where the sea borders the land are rich habitats. Coastal ecosystems exist along sandy beaches, rocky shores, and at cliffs that rise above crashing waves.

Here live mammals who may spend some time on land but whose diet comes from the sea. Here also live water birds who nest on shore but swim and dive for their food. And in the waters live fish, invertebrates, and plants on which these animals feed.

One spectacular marine mammal of the coldest northern waters is the **polar bear**. Because you've seen polar bears in zoos rather than in aquariums, you might think they are land animals. In the wild, they do sometimes come ashore, and females den for a few months in caves of ice to give birth and nurse their cubs. But most of the time, polar bears live on floes, or floating ice packs, in the Arctic Ocean. Adult males have even been seen on huge floes hundreds of miles from land.

They are not dependent on land for their diet, which consists primarily of fish, seals, and immature walruses. On shore, they might eat grasses, roots, and whatever land creatures they can catch—ground birds, arctic foxes, perhaps caribou. In captivity, their diet is primarily mackerel, some-

These polar bears' large, open zoo enclosure resembles the tundra of their natural habitat, an Alaskan coast. They can also swim in their eleven-foot-deep saltwater pond.

times dropped into the water so they can dive for it. Some zoo polar bears also get chicken or other fish as a treat.

These huge carnivores are seven to ten feet long and weigh 700 to over 1000 pounds. Their front paws are partially webbed to give them extra power in swimming, and all four feet have nonskid soles, covered with stiff, short hairs that provide good traction for running on ice. Polar bears can run as fast as twenty-five miles an hour.

In spite of their massive bulk, polar bears swim gracefully. Good zoos provide them with deep pools, and at some, such as the Central Park Zoo in New York City and the Point Defiance Zoo & Aquarium in Tacoma, Washington, there are viewing windows where visitors can watch them underwater, pirouetting like dancers. Though they are supremely adapted to the extreme cold of their native waters close to the North Pole, in zoos they manage to beat the heat in summer by spending their time in the pools.

Newborn polar bears weigh only one or two pounds—amazingly tiny, considering the size of their parents. A mother polar bear is fiercely protective of her babies, which is just as well, since in the wild a male might eat them if he got a chance. In a zoo, a pregnant female is provided with an isolated "ice cave" in which to give birth and nurse her cubs in private.

Polar bears are not especially afraid of humans and can be dangerous. Zookeepers are extremely cautious around them. On a few occasions, zoo visitors have ignored fences and warning signs and have gone too close to the bears and been killed.

Most zoos that exhibit polar bears have between two and four, usually females with perhaps one male. Very young males can live in a zoo habitat together, but not mature males. However, if you see a lone polar bear in a zoo, you don't have to feel sorry for it. In the wild, males and females come together at mating time, and females stay with their cubs until they are grown. But otherwise, both males and females are normally solitary.

Polar bears are an endangered species and are protected from sport hunters in many countries. In some places, however, such as the Northwest Territories of Canada, they are hunted for their pelts.

Humane Society of the United States

It is now against the law to keep polar bears in small, bare cages such as these, but some inferior zoos do it anyway.

When the Exxon oil company's tanker *Valdez* ran aground in 1989, spilling eleven million gallons of black, sticky crude oil into the clear waters of Prince William Sound, Alaska, hundreds of thousands of oil-soaked animals and birds died. That one oil spill alone ruined an area larger than the state of Delaware. Among the victims were sea otters

Sea otters are aquatic members of the weasel family, which includes minks, ferrets, and skunks. They have no layer of fat to insulate them against cold, but depend for warmth on their thick fur, which they groom daily. If their fur becomes coated with oil, they can freeze to death—or, when they try to clean themselves, they swallow the oil on their fur and are poisoned. After the *Valdez* disaster, rescue workers set up emergency stations and worked hard to save as many wildlife victims as they could. Professionals from four major west coast aquariums went to Alaska and participated in the enormous task of cleaning, treating, and nursing survivors. They were able to save a few hundred. Some of the sea otters were taken to aquariums.

Life for these furry brown animals has always been difficult. Few species have come so close to extinction yet managed to survive. Sea otters once inhabited an arc-shaped range that included the coastal waters of California, Canada, Alaska, the Aleutian Islands, Russia, and the northernmost island of Japan. But in the eighteenth and nineteenth centuries, they were ruthlessly hunted for their soft fur until, in the nick of time, the hunting was stopped by international treaty.

Even with no human interference, sea otters face many dangers in the wild. Sharks, killer whales, and eagles attack them or their pups; they often suffer from disease, accidents, and starvation; and in their rugged habitat they may be killed by severe storms or trapped in ice formations.

And today their habitats are threatened not only by oil spills but by offshore gas and oil drilling. At present, oil companies are pressuring for the right to explore for oil in many offshore waters, including our only remaining coastal wilderness, the Arctic National Wildlife Refuge, in Alaska. Even

When a sea otter feeds, it floats on its back and places a flat stone on its belly to use in cracking open shellfish for its dinner.

if oil were found there, it would meet U.S. needs for only a few months—but this magnificent part of our planet would be gone forever.

Sea otters are drowned accidentally in fish nets, poachers trap them for their pelts, boaters run over them, and shellfishermen kill them because they consider the otters a nuisance. The sea otters' main diet is shellfish—clams, crabs, abalone, and the like—and California shellfishermen complain that the otters take away their livelihood. To placate the fishermen, wildlife agencies have sometimes trapped and moved the otters to other locations, with mixed results. Many otters have either come back home or disappeared, possibly dying from the stress of capture and relocation.

Sea otters are three to four feet long, with short legs. While they are strong and graceful swimmers, using their tails and webbed hind feet for locomotion, they are clumsy on land and vulnerable to predators. They spend most of their time in the water, swimming or floating on their backs. They even eat and sleep in this position, anchoring themselves in beds of kelp (seaweed) to keep from drifting.

In the wild, adult male and female sea otters live apart, except during the breeding season. A female gives birth in the water, in a kelp bed, usually to just one pup, which she carries on her stomach in the water for about six weeks. Then she teaches the pup to dive for food and, after eight months or so, to live independently.

The sea otter is rare, both in the wild and in captivity. In an effort to help this threatened species survive, the Monterey Bay, Point Defiance, and Vancouver aquariums have breeding colonies of sea otters. The animals live in naturalistic habitats and dine on shellfish. The aquariums report that it costs $10,000 a year to keep each sea otter in its daily diet of twelve to fifteen pounds of shellfish!

You can see the sea otter's popular relative, the river otter, in many zoos and aquariums. People love to watch those playful animals, who often amuse themselves by sliding down the mud banks into the water of their freshwater habitat.

If an aquarium or zoo were to ask visitors to vote for their favorite sea bird, the penguin would surely win the contest. There are many species. Most are between one and two feet tall, but all are basically black and white and look as if they're dressed in tuxedos. Highly social, they stand around together on shore or sometimes line up like children on a diving board to dive into the water.

Wild penguins are found only in the southern hemisphere. Some species such as the emperor and Adélie inhabit the rocky beaches of lands that circle the South Pole. Others—the Humboldt, Magellanic, black, and Galapagos—live on the temperate coasts of South America.

The Humboldt penguin (sometimes called the Peruvian penguin) is named for the Humboldt ocean current, which flows north along this penguin's only range, the west coast of South America. The mainstay of its diet is anchovies, which puts it in direct competition with the fishermen of Peru's vast anchovy fishing fleets. Like all animals who must compete with humans for their food or habitat, the Humboldt penguins are losing. But they are being bred in the Species Survival Plan at such zoos as the Brookfield, the Saint Louis, and the Woodland Park, and in aquariums like the Vancouver.

Penguins eat mainly fish, squid, and crustaceans. They communicate in loud squawks and trumpeting calls; one species is even named the jackass penguin! The penguins who live in the temperate climate nest in burrows. Some zoos provide their penguins with fiberglass caves or boxes containing gravel or sand for them to dig their burrows in.

Seals eat penguins when they can catch them, but oil spills present an even greater threat. Many penguin colonies lie near tanker routes. Thousands of Magellanic penguins have died in oil spills in the Strait of Magellan, at the southern tip of South America.

Penguins can't fly, and they walk with a sort of comical waddle. They also flop on their bellies and toboggan on the snow, pushing themselves along with their wings. But when it comes to swimming, penguins are experts. On the surface, they paddle like ducks, but most of the time they zoom around underwater, flapping their wings as if flying and using their feet and tail as a rudder. Some species are able to dive as deep as eight hundred feet and stay underwater for over fifteen minutes.

Because people love to watch these birds swim, many newer aquariums and zoos keep them in cold, naturalistic habitats behind glass, with underwater viewing

Chuck Dresner/Saint Louis Zoo

One hope for the highly endangered Humboldt, or Peruvian, penguins is that they are being bred in the Species Survival Plan.

Despite their plump bodies, small wings, and short tails, puffins are good flyers and swimmers.

windows. Penguins adapt well to living in captivity and are tolerant of their keepers. When a keeper goes into their exhibit, they maintain a little distance, but they don't get upset or try to attack.

At the top of the earth, another sea bird, the **puffin**, swims in the arctic waters or roosts on the cliffs above them. Unlike penguins, puffins can fly. But like penguins, they also use their wings to give themselves speed when swimming underwater. Their plump black-and-white bodies are about nine inches long, their thick beaks colorful—in fact, puffins are sometimes called sea parrots. They have webbed orange-red feet.

Puffins eat fish, crustaceans, sand eels, herring, and a variety of tiny marine organisms called plankton. They nest in colonies on the bare rock ledges or in shallow burrows among the cliff grasses. A female usually lays only one egg, and her mate helps incubate the egg and feed the chick.

Many zoos and aquariums have either the common puffin, also called the Atlantic, or its relative of the northern Pacific, the tufted puffin, which sports long yellow feathers on its head. You'll find puffins in exhibits called Sea Birds, Rocky Shores, Ice Pack, Sea Cliffs, and the like, always with water and sometimes behind glass windows.

The National Aquarium in Baltimore acquired its common puffins about ten years ago as chicks. They are aloof with their keeper and hate to

40

be touched or picked up, though they will eat from her hand. The puffins accept her as a part of their environment.

The swirling waters of the California coast are the habitat of a bright-colored fish that's sometimes called the ocean goldfish. The garibaldi, named by an Italian fisherman for an Italian patriot, lives in the beds or "forests" of kelp, the giant seaweed that grows as tall as trees.

The garibaldi is very territorial and will fiercely defend its nest and habitat in the California coastal waters.

Garibaldis are from eight to about fourteen inches long, with large scales and spines on their dorsal, or back, fins. Newly hatched garibaldis are even more colorful than their parents, with dots and streaks of shiny blue on their golden scales.

When a male wants to attract a female, he cultivates a big patch of red algae (plantlike marine organisms). Unless a female thinks the patch is big enough and red enough, she won't lay her eggs there.

The California kelp forests support a whole range of aquatic life. Kelp is also harvested for use in many products. In fact, plants that live in water are necessary to all living things, for they help supply the earth with oxygen.

Many aquariums have kelp forest exhibits, and while most use imitation kelp, the Monterey Bay Aquarium has an outstanding forest of real kelp. This huge exhibit is sixty-six feet long and three stories high and contains an entire living community. Visitors can see it from various levels: from the first floor as if they were standing on the ocean's bottom, from a balcony, or from the second floor that's near the water surface.

Among the warm-blooded animals that inhabit the coastal waters of the Pacific ocean is a group called the pinnipeds, which means "wing-footed" or "fin-footed," and includes the walruses, seals, and sea lions. Scientists

Sea lions are highly social animals and gather in crowds on shores for mating or, as they are doing in this zoo habitat, just sunbathing.

believe the early ancestors of the pinnipeds lived on land and were related to bearlike creatures. In their flippers you can see the remains of legs and feet. Their front flippers even have five fingers with claws.

The seals and sea lions resemble each other; in fact, sea lions are known as eared seals—most species of seals have only slits for ears, but sea lions have little pointed ears. Seals are hunted traditionally for their pelts. Sea lions are not furred, but their skins can be made into leather. They are also slaughtered for food and for the oil of their fat.

While seals are rather helpless on land, sea lions get around because they can turn their hind flippers forward and hoist themselves along. They are intelligent and inquisitive. The trained "seals" that you see performing in aquariums, zoos, and circuses are actually sea lions.

Most aquariums and zoos have exhibits of sea lions, usually the California species, whose natural habitat extends from British Columbia to the Galapagos Islands. California sea lions are blackish brown and relatively small, five to eight feet long, and have a loud, honking bark.

These animals are fast swimmers and have been clocked at twenty-five miles per hour. When underwater, they can close their nostrils tight and dive to over 300 feet. They can leap out of water to a rock or platform five feet above. Their only natural enemies are sharks and killer whales.

The greatest threat to sea lions and seals is overfishing of their habitats by humans, who take the food the animals live on. Oil spills also kill vast numbers of them, as does ordinary household garbage that's dumped into coastal waters and landfills. Thousands of sea lions, seals, otters, and sea birds suffer and die every year from stuff we humans throw away without a thought to the creatures that will be harmed. Almost 100 million pounds of nondegradable plastics go into the ocean every year. Most of this garbage will never disappear.

Sometimes injured or orphaned sea lions have been found on U.S. west coast beaches and brought to aquariums for help. The aquariums' veterinarians and staff have nursed them, and if they lived, released them back into the sea.

California sea lions produce young quite readily in aquariums and zoos. They need shallow water to give birth in, so their exhibit must have a shore or sloping rock shelf. Also, they teach their pups to swim, so until the pups become skilled swimmers, they need a shallow beach for getting in and out of the water.

Sea lions are so trainable and attractive, they are often made to look like clowns and to perform in ridiculous ways. When a sea lion has to wear a hat, play a musical instrument, brush its teeth, and do silly tricks to make people laugh, we are being given the wrong message about these wonderful creatures.

George Antonelis/National Marine Fisheries Service

Many marine animals are killed by plastic six-pack holders for cans and bottles. Animals get their heads caught in them and strangle, or they drown in their struggles to free themselves.

Animals of the Coral Reefs

Coral reefs are showcases for some of the wonders of ocean life—and much more. They are delicately balanced ecosystems, the center of life for near-shore temperate waters all over the world. They provide food, nesting, and shelter for thousands of species of fish, shellfish, sea turtles, and other marine creatures.

Some coral reefs extend for many miles, acting as barriers that protect land masses. Australia's Great Barrier Reef is 1250 miles long! Many islands are actually coral reefs that were pushed up out of the sea hundreds of years ago.

Coral is an invertebrate animal, a tiny cylinder with arms or tentacles at one end. It lives in colonies with other corals, each individual animal attaching itself to some stationary surface like a rock or another coral and forming a hard cup around itself. When it dies, it leaves its rocky "skeleton," which other corals attach themselves to. This process goes on, with more and more corals cementing themselves to the skeletons of other corals, growing in various shapes—branches, organ pipes, staghorns, fans, mushrooms, and so on. One common type of coral colony is rounded and wrinkled and known as brain coral. When enough corals grow together, their hard, rocklike skeletons form reefs. A reef is made up of millions of tiny coral skeletons, along with millions of living corals.

Today, coral reefs the world over are dying. Oceangoing vessels plow through them, boats drag their anchors over them, divers break off pieces to sell or keep as souvenirs, and of course oil spills destroy them. Even the destruction of forests kills coral reefs, because soil containing natural nitrogen, agricultural fertilizers, and sewage runs off the bare land into rivers that empty into

A golden butterfly fish from the Red Sea lives in schools with others of its kind and feeds on plankton (tiny crustaceans) and bits of living coral. Some adults are as big as dinner plates.

coastal waters. Plantlike organisms called algae thrive in water containing those substances and crowd out the coral.

In the Philippines, divers gathering tropical fish to sell to collectors also kill coral reefs. Armed with squirt bottles containing cyanide, a poison, they shoot into the living reefs. Stunned fish float from the reef, so helpless they can be captured by hand. Survivors are sold to private tropical fish collectors all over the world.

Not only is the reef killed by the cyanide, but the fish often die from the stress of capture and transport. Those that live long enough to end up in a hobby aquarium often suffer liver damage from the cyanide and die within six months. Three-quarters of the tropical fish taken from coral reefs die within a year. Conservationists now urge people who keep tropical fish as a hobby to buy only those that are captive-bred or caught by nets.

Some efforts to protect the world's coral reefs are under way, and hopefully they will succeed before it is too late.

Almost all large public aquariums have coral reef exhibits. The coral may be living or dead, or possibly, if certain shapes are desired, man-made, which looks so real you can't tell the difference. Such exhibits demonstrate why this exquisite ecosystem should not become an underwater desert.

Angelfish are among the prettiest reef fish in aquariums. They are about ten inches long on average and come in a variety of beautiful colors and patterns; they have names such as regal, emperor, princess, queen, French, and bluefaced angelfish. In their natural habitats—the Red Sea and the Australian Great Barrier Reef—they stick close to the reefs and nibble on sponges, living corals, and vegetation. In an aquarium, angelfish are fed algae, tiny fish, bits of sponge, and vegetables. Some angelfish like peas!

In the balance of life in a coral reef, there are predators and prey. One predator, the lionfish, has few enemies and is totally unafraid, even of human divers. It is covered with spines five to six inches long that act like hypodermic needles, injecting venom from glands at the spines' base. The venom can badly hurt, even kill, a person who touches or steps on one of these fish. Lionfish are treated with respect by the aquarists who take care of them.

These fish have big appetites. In the wild, they eat small fish, though in captivity they will also eat raw meat. In an aquarium, they need cover such

This regal angelfish feeds on tiny organisms living among the mushroom coral and delicate elegance coral in its naturalistic exhibit.

as corals or plants, and lots of space to swim in. Lionfish are usually kept alone or with fish larger than themselves.

Sea anemones (a-nem-a-nees) have been called flowers of the sea, but they are not plants. They are invertebrates, living in all oceans warm and cold, from shallow zones to depths of six or more miles. However, most, and certainly the prettiest, live in warmer waters, especially on coral reefs.

There are over a thousand sea anemone species, varying in size from less than an inch to nearly five feet and growing in every shape imaginable. They attach themselves to coral, rocks, seashells, and wharfs and usually stay there, waving their tentacles in the ocean currents. They are preyed upon by some species of eels, sea stars, fish, and sea slugs.

But anemones are carnivores, and though they don't swim, they feed themselves by waiting until a prey fish swims close. When the fish touches the anemone's tentacles, it receives a sting that paralyzes it. Then the anemone can maneuver the prey into its mouth.

Certain crabs make use of the anemone's stinging ability. They carry anemones in their claws and when threatened, thrust the anemones into

David Cupp / Scripps Aquarium-Museum

A young lionfish is already capable of delivering a venomous sting with its needle-sharp spines.

This little male tomato clown fish makes his home among the tentacles of a green sea anemone. Female tomato clowns are black, and larger than the males.

the face of their attackers. A hermit crab may carry an anemone on its shell house; when it outgrows that shell and has to move to a larger one, the hermit crab takes its anemone along and transplants it to the new shell.

More than fifty species of fish are immune to the anemone's poison and spend all or part of their lives living among the tentacles of tropical species. One, the clown fish, is found living with anemones of the Pacific and Indian oceans.

Clown fish develop in an unusual way. Most unborn creatures begin life with both male and female characteristics, and then become one or the other before birth. But clown fish are all male when hatched! Gradually those that grow larger and more dominant turn into females.

A clown fish takes up residence within an anemone and eats, sleeps, even lays its eggs there. This fish feeds on food particles that it picks from the corners of the anemone's mouth, and in turn it places bits of food within reach of the anemone. It is even said to lure other fish into the anemone's tentacles. The clown fish and the anemone have a perfect symbiotic relationship, which means they are dependent on, and benefit from, each other.

In any aquarium's coral reef or tropical waters exhibit, you will find many anemones. Look for the little fish that live among their tentacles.

Animals of the Offshore Open Seas

The oceans and seas of the earth are all connected with one another in a single, big saltwater system. Compared to other ecosystems, the mid-ocean, where the water is deepest and light cannot penetrate, has relatively few animals living in it. But the waters offshore from the land masses, blending with but extending just beyond the coastal waters, are filled with life.

Within each hemisphere, ocean currents circulate from the North and South poles to the warm-water regions of the equator and back again. Ecosystems of the land differ from those of the oceans in that the warmest land habitats support the most plant and animal life. The warm, moist rain forests, for example, have more plants and creatures than all other regions, while the frozen tundra of the Arctic or highest mountaintops have fewer.

It's just the opposite in the oceans and seas. Sea water that is relatively warm and calm contains many, many types of organisms, but fewer than cold water. Water in cold, stormy regions is often heaving with waves; therefore it contains a lot of oxygen and also churns up nourishing plant and animal matter from the bottom.

Because the seas are connected, some marine creatures adapt to several or all of them, appearing in different species of the same biological family. One such animal is the sea star, or starfish. Not a fish but a type of invertebrate called an echinoderm, meaning spiny-skinned, the sea star is a bottom dweller in every ocean of the world. Sea stars live in tidal pools, on sandy shores, or in cool dark waters five miles down. At an aquarium, you'll find sea stars in many exhibits, especially in a tide pool or touch pool exhibit, where you can usually pick them up.

There are over 18,000 species, ranging in size from several inches to nearly two feet across. Most have five rays or arms, but there are species with over twenty. Sea stars vary widely in color and texture, and they have been given names such as sunflower, leather, crown of thorns, morning sun, even cookie.

Sea stars are predators with large appetites; they eat fish, shellfish, and other invertebrates, even one another. They capture their prey with little suction cups on the bottoms of their arms, which are strong enough to pry open the shells of clams and oysters. Most sea stars can push their stom-

David Cupp/Monterey Bay Aquarium

The large sunflower sea star, a fierce predator, is a bottom dweller in the offshore seas of the North American Pacific coast.

achs inside out through their mouths, wrap their stomachs around their prey, and digest their food on the outside. In an aquarium, they are fed mainly snails, though sometimes if a fish or invertebrate dies, its carcass is offered to the sea stars.

A sea star has an astonishing ability to regenerate. This means that if you cut off one of its arms, it will grow another. What's more, the cut-off arm will grow into a whole new sea star!

———

When you think of a shark, what probably comes to mind is the huge, awesome-looking fish with a mouthful of teeth. The big species such as the hammerhead, tiger, white, and blue are especially ferocious hunters and dangerous to human swimmers. Almost every aquarium has at least some sharks on exhibit, and people get a scary thrill out of looking at them.

There are about 150 species of sharks. One you'll often find in aquariums is the **leopard shark**, a member of a relatively small group sometimes called dogfish. It feeds on small fish, worms, shellfish, and crustaceans in the offshore waters along the Pacific coast from Oregon to Baja California.

Sharks tend to be darker colored on the top of their bodies, so that if seen from above, they blend with the ocean floor below them. And they're lighter colored along their bottom, so that creatures swimming below have a harder time seeing them against the sky. This coloration helps in hunting their prey.

These animals can swim fast, but only fast-forward, not in reverse. They also can't pause or hover—if they stop swimming, they sink. Although they aren't intelligent, they hunt very effectively using their senses of vision and smell and what's called electrolocation. This means they use special organs to detect the electric fields produced by the movements of creatures they prey upon.

Instead of laying eggs like most other fish, sharks are live-bearers, animals that give birth to living young. Infant sharks are born fully developed, little miniatures of the adults, and don't require any care from the mother. You might see a tankful of baby sharks in an aquarium.

David Cupp/Monterey Bay Aquarium

The leopard shark is small for a shark, not much over three feet long. It prefers to swim along sandy or muddy offshore bottoms.

To scrub and vacuum the tanks containing sharks, keepers wearing wet suits net the sharks to one side of the tank. One keeper cleans the tank while the helper keeps an eye on the sharks to be sure none escapes from the net.

In the wild, sharks often eat carrion, the carcasses of dead animals; this helps to keep their habitat clean. In an aquarium, keepers feed sharks by putting fish on long poles and waving them in front of the sharks. Some won't eat fish if it has been frozen, insisting on fresh. Keepers know their sharks by name or number and keep track of what food and how much each one eats.

The warm-blooded, air-breathing mammals that live entirely in water are called cetaceans (se-tay-shuns): whales, dolphins, and porpoises. The word "porpoise" was formerly used interchangeably with "dolphin," but a porpoise is actually a different animal.

Dolphins and whales have large brains. In the wild, they live together in kinship groups, usually called pods, which are like extended families. They cooperate with one another, call to one another, and if one gets in trouble, members of its group will come to its aid. Mothers are intensely protective of their young, who stay with them for several years. It is cruel, and in fact now illegal, to keep any cetacean alone in captivity.

Most cetaceans are cold-water animals. They eat nutrients churned up from the sea bottom, especially tiny shrimplike creatures called krill, the main diet of whales. Cetaceans are powerful swimmers. Unlike fish, who propel themselves through the water by moving their tails back and forth, cetaceans move their tails up and down. They can hold their breath underwater for long lengths of time, breathing voluntarily rather than automatically like humans do. They breathe through a blowhole on top of their heads, which they keep tightly closed when they are underwater.

Whales are generally peaceful and do not harm humans unless they are attacked. However, they have been hunted relentlessly for thousands of years, for food and products made from their bodies. Now, even though most whale products have been replaced by other, more easily available materials, some nations, particularly Japan, Norway, South Korea, and the Philippines, still hunt them.

Dolphins are slaughtered by fishermen who say the animals compete for fish; Japanese fishermen have driven thousands of them onto beaches and harpooned them in bloody massacres. And like all aquatic creatures, cetaceans are subject to poisoning from chemical wastes and human trash that are dumped in offshore waters.

In recent years, a major killer of all marine animals is the use of drift nets, particularly by Japanese, Taiwanese, and Korean fishermen. These are huge nets of almost invisible plastic webbing that stretch for up to fifteen miles and hang forty feet deep in the water. The so-called gill nets are similar but smaller. These "curtains of death" catch whole schools of fish—and anything else that has the misfortune to swim into them. Every year they kill, either by

Twilly Cannon/Greenpeace

This dolphin, like so many other marine animals, became entangled and drowned in a gill net, a type widely used in commercial fishing.

drowning or by mutilation, unknown thousands, perhaps millions, of dolphins, turtles, pinnipeds, otters, and sea birds that become entangled in them.

Fishermen also carelessly discard used nets, which continue to drift through the waters forever, killing as they go. Environmentalists, conservationists, and animal rights groups are actively protesting the use of drift nets and gill nets.

While most of the land-dwelling animals you see in zoos today have been born in captivity, this is not true of whales and dolphins. They don't readily reproduce in captivity; if females do give birth, many of the calves die. But there is a demand for dolphins and small whales in aquariums, so most are taken from the wild.

Capture is a terrible ordeal for any wild animal, especially for those that live in strong kinship groups. Many cetaceans die in captivity, even in fairly good aquariums. They die from stress soon after capture, or refuse to eat, possibly from loneliness at being separated from their fellows. Some develop stress-related illnesses, such as stomach ulcers, from being confined in tanks that are too small or subject to noise and vibrations from pumps and filters.

An impressive cetacean that some aquariums exhibit is the orca, better known as the killer whale, though most scientists classify it as a large dolphin rather than a true whale. It is black and white, twenty-five to thirty feet long, weighs as much as six tons, and has a rounded head and sharp teeth.

In the wild, orcas are unique among cetaceans in that they hunt in well-organized packs and eat fish, seals, small dolphins, and even whales, though none are known to have killed humans. Orcas are accustomed to cruising as much as 50 to 100 miles a day. Being confined to a tank must be very hard on them.

Because of their intelligence, cetaceans such as orcas, bottlenose dolphins, and beluga (white) whales can be trained to perform amazing tricks. But sometimes an aquarium puts great pressure on the animals—and on

These captive orcas live in a million gallons of filtered seawater with oceanlike waves.

the trainers—so that the animals will earn their keep in a hurry. A few years ago, several trainers at Sea World of California were injured, two of them seriously, by orcas who apparently objected to being rushed into performing.

When a popular performing cetacean dies, the facility that owns it usually just obtains another and gives it the same name as the one that died. The public never knows the difference. At Sea World, you might see a performing orca named Shamu, but there have been many Shamus, one after the other.

Some aquarists say that captive whales and dolphins are better off having something to do, rather than enduring the boredom of just swimming in circles. Many of the tricks they are trained to do are based on behavior that the animals do naturally.

But when they are made to be pets or clowns, we are misled about these magnificent wild animals. It is natural for them to leap out of the water, for example, but it is nonsense to pretend that they leap up to "kiss" their trainer. It is necessary to train a captive dolphin to place its tail on the dock so blood can be drawn when the veterinarian wants to check on its health. But in some silly dolphin shows, the animal is made to present its tail to be "spanked" for "misbehaving," while the unthinking audience roars with laughter. At some aquariums, such as Ocean World in Florida, dolphins have died from being kept in small petting pools. The "smile" that bottlenose dolphins, orcas, and beluga whales seem to wear, by the way, is really just the way their mouths are shaped, not an expression of happiness.

One argument that's often given in favor of exhibiting cetaceans is that by seeing these wonderful animals in real life, we are more likely to care about their fate in the wild. Maybe so. But many people think it is wrong for humans to deprive them of their freedom, separate them from their kinfolk, put them in tanks, and make them do tricks for their food, simply to amuse us. The Monterey Bay Aquarium has chosen instead to display only life-size models of marine mammals, including a replica of a forty-three-foot gray whale, along with truly educational graphics and videos that show them in their natural habitats.

Cetaceans in captivity should have at least a million gallons of interesting, varied space with rocks underwater, channels, sand bars, and waves. In recent years, some of the better aquariums have built new, interesting marine mammal habitats that are much larger than the previous standard size. The Brookfield Zoo, in Chicago, has created a new dolphinarium that is three times larger than the tanks its three dolphins lived in for years. The Shedd Aquarium, also in Chicago, has a new Oceanarium, a huge two-million-gallon naturalistic pool, for several dolphins and small whales. The Indianapolis Zoo's Waters Complex includes a two-million-gallon pavilion for its dolphins.

But some aquariums still keep cetaceans in plain concrete swimming pools. As the public learns more about wildlife, it has higher expectations of aquariums and zoos. Perhaps the inferior places will go out of business because nobody will visit them.

It is fitting to end this book with a marine invertebrate, since invertebrates so greatly outnumber all the rest of us on our water planet. They range in size from creatures so small that you need a microscope to see them, up to the large arctic jellyfish that's 240 feet long.

Many people would probably agree that the most fantastic invertebrate in all the seas is the octopus. It is a mollusk, an invertebrate with a relatively soft body. Many mollusks—clams, oysters, snails—have protective shells, but the octopus does not. Its body is shaped like a bag, from which eight long arms radiate. It is a predator and eats mainly shellfish and crabs. The bite of most octopus species is toxic.

Octopuses live on the bottom of most temperate offshore waters. They vary in size from a few inches long to more than thirty feet. There is a lot of folklore about the big ones. Horror movies with scenes of underwater diving often show somebody pretending to fight off an attack from a monster

David Cupp/Monterey Bay Aquarium

An octopus has a double row of suckers on each of its arms, which it uses in capturing and holding its prey. A giant Pacific octopus like this one could be 30 feet long.

octopus. But in truth, these animals are fairly shy except in pursuing their prey. When frightened, they expel an inky cloud as protective cover while they escape. They shelter in caves and in the crevices of rocks.

If you can imagine arm-wrestling with sixteen arms, that's what the courtship behavior of a male and female octopus looks like. They also show vivid changes of color to attract each other.

A female octopus breeds only once and lays huge amounts of eggs, as many as a thousand in clusters like grapes. She may string them around her cave or hold them in her arms, spraying them with streams of water to keep them clean and supplied with oxygen. While the eggs are incubating, for about two months, she doesn't leave her vigil even to eat. After her eggs hatch, the exhausted female dies.

Aquarists say that octopuses are as intelligent as many mammals. They can learn and remember. They're a challenge to keep in an aquarium, because they've been known to crawl out of their tanks, perhaps out of sheer curiosity or perhaps trying to find a way back to the sea. They can carry enough water in their bodies to supply them with oxygen for short periods out of water.

A giant Pacific octopus at the Scripps Aquarium-Museum once amazed everyone with its ingenuity. It was kept in a tank near an exhibit with many kinds of fish. The staff of the aquarium kept noticing that, from time to time, fish were missing. One night, a watchman caught the thief in the act. The octopus crawled out of its tank, slithered across the floor, hitched itself up the side of the fishes' tank, caught and ate a few fish—and then crawled back home to its own tank. This is a true story.

However, today at most aquariums, octopuses' tanks are lined around the top with Astroturf, a kind of all-weather carpeting that the animals can't attach their suckers to. So, visitors and staff are not likely to see an octopus anywhere but in its tank.

What To Look For
in an Aquatic Exhibit

1. How naturalistic is the exhibit? Is it designed to imitate the wild habitat? Or, are the animals just in a plain tank or bare cage with a concrete pool?

2. If the exhibit is behind glass, is it situated so people can't bang on the glass? Sounds are magnified behind glass, and can scare or annoy the animals.

3. If the exhibit has a pool, is it designed so people can't throw coins in the water? Some animals swallow coins and can become sick or die. Also, the coins make the exhibit look trashy.

4. Is the water clean, with no garbage floating in it? Is the area around the pool clean?

5. Is the pool deep, with tunnels and rocks where the animals can get away if they want privacy?

6. If the exhibit is outdoors, do the animals have both sun and shade?

7. If the animals are social creatures, like dolphins, whales, otters, and pinnipeds, do they have companions of their own kind?

8. If the animals have to perform, do they display their natural abilities, or are they made to look silly?

9. Are there signs near the exhibit that tell you about the animals and their natural habitats?

Index

Page numbers in *italics* refer to photographs.